MW00877016

A Horse For Ella

Elizabeth A Reeves

©2012 Elizabeth A Reeves

Cover photo gorilla at

depositphotos.com

A Horse for Ella

For Ella Lewis

Ella loved horses. She loved their pretty manes. She loved their bright eyes.

Ella had a room full of horses. She had pictures of horses on the walls. She had toy horses. Mom even made her horse pancakes.

But Ella was not happy. She wanted her very own horse.

"Please, can I have a horse?" She asked.

"A horse is a lot of work," said Dad.

"A horse eats a lot of food," said Mom.

"I can feed a horse," Ella said. "I can work hard. Can I have a horse?"

Mom and Dad took Ella to a farm. There were lots of horses everywhere.

"Wow," Ella said. "Are we going to buy a horse?"

"Not yet," said Dad. He smiled. "First, we will work."

A woman gave Dad a shovel. Mom got a cart.

"The stalls are dirty," Mom said. "We must clean them."

Dad got straw. Mom and Ella took out the dirty straw. They put clean straw in the stalls.

Ella was tired. "Can I get a horse now?" She asked.

"Not yet," said Dad.

"There is more work to do," said Mom.

"More work?" Ella asked.

"Yes," Mom said.

"We must clean the saddles and bridles," Dad said.

"We need to brush and feed the horses," said Mom.

"And fill the water buckets," Dad said.

Ella was so tired. "If I clean and feed and brush, then can I have a horse?"

"Not yet," said Mom. "There is still so much to do."

Ella washed buckets. She filled the buckets with water. She put the buckets in every stall so the horses could drink.

Dad and Mom helped Ella use soap to clean the saddles and bridles for the horses. The bubbles got everywhere. It was fun. The clean leather smelled good.

Ella brushed the horses. There were lots of brushes. There were brushes for the mane and tail of the horse. There were brushes for the body of the horse. There was a soft brush for faces.

Ella liked to brush horses.

Ella and Mom and Dad carried hay into all of the stalls. The horses liked to eat hay. They were happy to have food. It made Ella happy to make them happy.

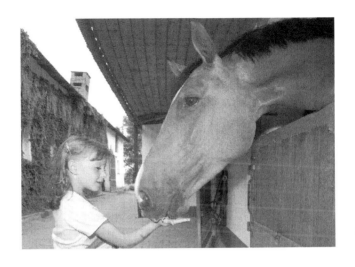

"Now, can I have a horse?" Ella asked.

"If you have a horse," Dad said. "You will have to do this every day."

"Every day?" Ella asked. She was very tired. She thought about all the work. She thought and thought. She was very sad. "It is a lot of work," she said. "But I really want a horse."

"I know," said Mom. "But I have an idea."

Mom held Ella's hand. They walked to a ring where lots of little girls like Ella were riding on ponies. They wore helmets and boots. They were having fun.

"These girls love horses, too," Mom said.

"They have their own horses," Ella said, sadly.

"No," Dad said. "They do not have horses. They are having a lesson."

"If you have riding lessons," Mom said. "You can be with horses. You will not have to work so hard."

"I will not have to work hard?" Ella asked.

"Yes," said Dad.

Ella thought. She loved horses. She did not love all the work.

"Can I have riding lessons?" Ella asked.

"Yes," said Mom.

"Yes," said Dad.

"I love horses," Ella said. "But they are a lot of work."

A Lesson For Ella

Ella had a riding lesson.

"Come on," she said to Dad. "I want to ride now!"

Dad smiled. "Do you have your boots?"

"Yes," said Ella.

"Do you have your helmet?" asked Mom.

"Yes," Ella said.

"Do you have an apple for the horse?" Dad asked.

"Yes," Ella said. "Now can we go? I want to ride."

"We can go now," said Mom.

Mom, Dad, and Ella drove to the barn. There were lots of horses.

Ella was excited. She jumped out of the car.

"Wait!" Mom shouted. "Do you have your helmet?"

Ella had forgotten her helmet in the car. "Oops," she said.

Ella got her helmet. "Why do I need a helmet?" She asked.

"Riders wear helmets so they can be safe," said Dad.

"If you fall off of the horse you will not hurt your head," Mom said.

Ella did not want to get hurt. "I do not want to fall," she said.

"If you do fall," Dad said, "you must get back on."

"Yes," Mom said.

Ella went to the barn. A pony was waiting for her.

"You will ride him today," said the lady. "His name is Big."

Ella laughed. "He is so small!"

"Yes," the lady said. "That is why we call him Big,"

Ella thought that was funny.

Ella put on her helmet. The lady helped her get up on Big.

"Wow," Ella said, "I feel very tall!"

"See?" The lady laughed. "He is Big."

"Yes," said Ella.

Big walked around the ring. It was fun. Ella wanted to ride Big all the time.

"I love Big," she said.

"It is time to trot," said the lady. "Trotting is when the horse jogs. It is very bumpy. You can hold his mane so you will not fall."

"I do not want to fall," said Ella. She was a little scared.

"If you do fall," the lady said. "You have to get back on."

Ella held Big's mane. Big started to trot. Trotting was very bouncy.

Ella laughed. She liked bouncing. She let go of Big's mane.

Big stopped.

Ella fell off. She did not land on her head. She landed on her bottom.

Ella stood up. "That did not hurt," she said. "I have to get back on."

"Yes," said the lady. She helped Ella get back on.

"I am glad I have my helmet," Ella said. "I need a helmet for my bottom."

About the Author

Bonnie Lewis is a former horse rescuer from Arizona. These days she can be found running after four sons, three dogs, and her two cats. Horses have always been a big part of her life and passions. She is also passionate about animal rescue.

She writes about strong, intelligent, self-sufficient heroines. She is the author of The Jumping Into Danger series and the new series Riding a Dead Horse, coming in 2013.

Made in the USA
Lexington, KY
11 October 2016